AN EID STORY

THE LOST RING

Fawzia Gilani-Williams

Illustrated by Kulthum Burgess

MUSLIM CHILDREN'S LIBRARY

THE EID STORIES SERIES

An Eid Story: The Lost Ring
Author: Fawzia Gilani-Williams
Illustrator: Kulthum Burgess
Book Design: S. Stratford

Published by
The Islamic Foundation
Markfield Conference Centre
Ratby Lane, Markfield
Leicestershire, LE67 9SY
United Kingdom
T: (01530) 244 944   F: (01530) 244 946
E: publications@islamic-foundation.com

Quran House, PO Box 30611, Nairobi, Kenya
PMB 3193, Kano, Nigeria

British Library Cataloguing in Publication Data

Gilani-Williams, Fawzia

　　The lost ring. - (An Eid story; 1) (Muslim children's library)
　　1. Fasts and feasts - Islam - Juvenile fiction 2. Rings -
　　Juvenile fiction 3. Children's stories
　　I. Title II. Burgess, Kulthum III. Islamic Foundation
　　(Great Britain) 823.9'2[J]

　　ISBN-13: 9780860375654

Printed by Proost International Book Production, Belgium

An Eid Story: The Lost Ring

Rahma's grandmother and cousin, Muslimah, were visiting for *Eid*. Grandma had sewn *Eid* dresses for both of the girls.

"Try them on to see if they fit," said Grandma. Rahma and Muslimah put on their long, pretty dresses and began twirling in the living room.

"We look like princesses, don't we, Grandma?" laughed Rahma.

Grandma looked up from kneading the dough and smiled.

"Masha' Allah! Both of you look wonderful. But change your clothes, so you don't spoil them," she advised.

After changing, Muslimah sat down at the kitchen table and watched her grandmother knead the dough with one hand.

"I have to use two hands now," smiled Grandma. Muslimah watched Grandma slip off her gold ring. She knew it was a special ring from Grandpa.

Just then, Rahma's mum and dad walked through the door. They had been busy with *Eid* shopping.

"As-Salamu 'Alaikum, Mum, Dad," called Rahma.

"As-Salamu 'Alaikum, Uncle Khalid and Auntie Farnaz!" greeted Muslimah.

"Wa-'Alaikum as-Salam, girls!" replied Rahma's parents.

"Did you have fun, Mummy?" asked Rahma.

"No, darling, I didn't. I'm so tired!" answered
Mum as she leant down to hug Rahma.
"I had fun though!" laughed Dad. "Going
shopping is a treat for me!" Rahma's dad was so
busy working at the hospital, he rarely had time to
go shopping.

When Mum went into the kitchen, she saw
Grandma preparing the dough for the *Eid samosas*.

"Oh Mother!" she exclaimed. "You should let me
do the cooking. I don't want you to get tired."

"I thought I would knead the dough for the
samosas," said Grandma. "But now that you are
back, I can give the children the gift that I bought
for them. It's called the Multi-Madrasa!"

"Oh! They'll like that," answered Mum. "Our
neighbour, Hashim, has that programme. It's very
exciting!"

Just then, Muslimah walked into the kitchen and
asked, "Auntie Farnaz, when are you going to
make the *samosas?* Rahma and I would like to help
you make them."

"In about an hour, darling!" replied Mum as she struggled upstairs, clutching several bags.

The children played with Grandma, while Dad hung *Eid* lights outside and around the doorway. Soon it was time for *Salat-ul-Zuhr*.

Rahma's brothers, Taha and Hamza, laid out a sheet on the floor for everyone to pray on. Then Hamza called the *Adhan* and Dad led the prayer. When everyone had finished the prayer, Grandma made some tea for the adults and hot chocolate for the children.

Meanwhile, Mum began to prepare the mixture for the *samosas*. She had neatly arranged plates of mashed potatoes, chopped green chillies, diced onions, spices and salt.

"Hmmm," wondered Mum. "Something's missing." She glanced at the ingredients again and then realized. "Ah, the peas!"

"Muslimah and Rahma, darling!" called Mum. "Are you ready to help me mix these ingredients? I'm just going to get the peas from the fridge." Rahma had been looking forward to doing the *samosas* all week. She loved to eat the hot and spicy Indian pastries. Both of the girls rushed to the bathroom to wash their hands.

Rahma got back to the kitchen counter first and stood on top of the footstool. She saw her grandmother's ring next to the bowl of dough. "Oooh! Grandma's ring!" she exclaimed. She put on the ring, but it was too large for her fingers so she put it on her thumb. Muslimah came and stood next to Rahma. Both of them gently prodded the dough. It looked like a big fluffy cloud.

Mum was back in the kitchen again. She emptied the peas into a big bowl. Then she added the rest of the ingredients to the mashed potatoes.

"Girls, did you wash your hands?" she asked.

Rahma and Muslimah nodded.

"Okay, who's first?" asked Mum.

"Rahma can be first because she's the youngest!" offered Muslimah.

"Thank you, Muslimah!" smiled Rahma.

Rahma put both of her hands into the bowl and began to squeeze the mixture together.

"Ooh! This feels so good, Muslimah," she laughed.

Soon it was Muslimah's turn. Rahma washed her
hands and then helped her mum roll the dough
into small circles.

While the girls worked, Mum told them about her
shopping trip.

When it was time to spoon the mixture onto the
rolled pieces of dough, Grandma came into the
kitchen and helped.

Rahma placed the last *samosa* in the storage container. "Well done, girls!" said Mum. "I'll put them in the freezer for now and *Insha' Allah*, we will fry them on *Eid* day."

"We need to clean and tidy up to welcome the blessed days of *Eid*," said Grandma. So, the family spent the rest of the afternoon vacuuming, mopping, dusting and washing. Everyone was tired by the end of the day. Finally, Dad sat down with the children to remind them about *Eid-ul-Adha*.

"Can anyone tell me the name of the *Eid* we have after Ramadan?" he asked.
"It's *Eid-ul-Fitr!*" exclaimed Muslimah.
"Masha' Allah!" said Dad. "Does anyone know the name of the *Eid* we're going to have?"
"Ooh, Dad! My teacher, Sister Nadia, told us last week. It is called *Eid-ul-Adha*, the Festival of Sacrifice!"

"Well done, Rahma," complimented Dad. "Some people call it the Big *Eid* too."

Dad told the family about the story of the Prophet Ibrahim and his family, and how willing he was to always obey Allah. "He had a great love for Allah," explained Dad, "and he had a great love for all people. We should try to be like the Prophet Ibrahim."

The children listened with excitement as Dad told them about how Allah had tested the Prophet Ibrahim's obedience and how the Prophet Ibrahim was willing to sacrifice even his beloved son, Ismail. But just when the moment came, Allah sent a ram to be sacrificed in place of Ismail.

"And that's why Muslims all over the world sacrifice goats, sheep, camels or cows on the day of *Eid-ul-Adha*," explained Dad. "To show that they will also be as obedient to Allah as the Prophets

Ibrahim and Ismail always were."

"The poor people are very happy on that day too, aren't they, Dad?" said Rahma.

"Yes, *Masha' Allah!* They are! On that day all the poor and needy people receive meat and gifts and there is so much love and kindness!" answered Dad.

"That's how Allah wants everyone to treat each other," said Grandma. "He wants us to be kind and loving and to share with everyone."

"Insha' Allah, tomorrow we will fast for the Day of *Arafat* and we can visit the sick children in the hospital and take some sweets for them," said Dad.

On the Day of *Arafat* the children were busy. They visited the hospital and took gifts to people in the community and to the neighbours.

Soon, it was time to break the fast. "Who would like to make a *du'a?"* asked Dad.
"Uncle Khalid, I learnt a good *du'a,* can I say it please?" asked Muslimah.
"Of course you can, Muslimah," smiled her uncle.
"May the many blessings of Allah reach everyone, may Allah give us peace and may Allah give everyone a very joyful and blessed *Eid, ameen,"* said Muslimah.

"*Ameen!*" said everyone.

"That's a beautiful *du'a*, Muslimah," smiled Grandma.

After *Salat-ul-Maghrib*, everyone finished their meal and then helped with the washing and cleaning. Then, they sat in the living room around Dad.

Dad went over the *sunnah* of the blessed Prophet Muhammad for *Salat-ul-Eid*.

"For *Eid-ul-Adha,* the *sunnah* is to eat after the prayer," explained Dad. *"Insha' Allah,* there will be some tasty treats at the *Eid Musalla.* This is where everyone meets to pray."

The children reminded each other of what Muslims do for *Eid*.

"Always have a bath – *ghusl* – make *wudu* and put your best clothes on," said Rahma.

"Give money, clothes and food to the poor," said Taha.

"And give a third of the meat to the poor and a third to friends and relatives," said Hamza.

"Wake up early," said Muslimah, "and pray, 'God is most Great. God is most Great. There is no one else worthy of worship except God and God is most Great. God is most Great and all praise is for God."

"*Masha' Allah!*" said Mum. "You are all so good! Well done for remembering all those things!"

That night the children found it very difficult to sleep. They were so excited.

Finally it was the day of *Eid*.

"Al-Hamdulillah!" said Rahma.

"Subhan Allah!" said Muslimah.

Everyone rushed around trying to get ready.

All the way to the *Eid Musalla,* everyone chanted the *Takbir-e-Tashriq*.

After *Salat-ul-Eid,* Dad went with his friends to a farm to choose a sheep for *Qurbani* – Sacrifice.

Finally, in the evening, after all the meat had been distributed and the *Eid* dinner cooked, the guests began to arrive. Every knock at the door was followed with a loud greeting of *Eid Mubarak!*

A little later in the evening, Grandma suddenly realized that she didn't have her ring!
"Oh! *Innalillah!* Maybe I dropped it at the *Eid* prayer!" she cried.

Everyone froze, they knew how much Grandma
loved her ring.

"No, Grandma," said Muslimah. "The last I
remember, you left the ring on the kitchen counter
when we were making the *samosas*. Don't worry,
Insha' Allah, we'll find it."

Grandma looked worried but said, *"Insha' Allah,* I hope it's here in the house."

Muslimah gathered all the children together. "Leave it to me!" said Hashim, who lived next door. "I'm a really good detective. The first thing we need to do is to question everybody." Suddenly, Rahma let out a huge gasp. *"Ya Allah!"* she exclaimed. Her eyes were wide open and her hands covered her face. "Oh no!" cried Rahma as she remembered wearing Grandma's ring. "The ring is in one of the *samosas!"* she stammered. The children looked at Rahma in disbelief. "What do you mean in the *samosas?"* asked Hashim. "How could the ring be in the *samosas?"* *"Subhan Allah!* It is!" insisted Rahma. "I was wearing Grandma's ring when I was helping to make the *samosas!"* "There's only one thing to do, we're going to have to open up all the *samosas* before eating them," said Hamza. "It's the only way!"

The children looked at the huge platter of *samosas* on the dining room table. Each child took a *samosa* to eat. One after the other, the children opened each *samosa* to check for the ring before eating it.

Mum came into the dining room for some napkins and looked at the children curiously.

"You like my *samosas,* huh?" she said, looking puzzled and raising her eyebrows.

All of the children were holding a *samosa* in their hands.

They all smiled and nodded.

Mum smiled back and nodded approvingly.

"Al-Hamdulillah!" she said. "But try some of the other food too!"

The children continued their task. Finally there was only one *samosa* left. Everyone was holding their stomach.

"I can't eat another bite!" cried Hamza.

Muslimah took the last *samosa* and broke it into four pieces.

"It's got to be in here!" she said. She gave Taha, Rahma and Hashim a piece each.

"It's not here!" each one cried in disbelief.

Rahma's face turned red, she looked like she was going to cry.

"That was Grandma's favourite ring, and now it's lost forever!" she wailed. Rahma felt miserable.

"I'll have to tell Mum and Grandma and ruin *Eid* for everyone," sniffed Rahma.

"Try not to worry, *Insha' Allah,* we'll find Grandma's ring," reassured Hamza.

"Come on," encouraged Muslimah, "let's all recite *Ayat-ul-Kursi* and ask for Allah's help."

After making *du'a* the children walked into the living room. The mothers were sitting in one area chatting about Good Faith School's fundraiser.

The fathers were by the fireplace talking about the problems of the world.

Just then, Mum let out a yell, "Ouch!" Everyone looked at Mum who was holding her jaw and a half eaten *samosa*.

"*Subhan Allah!* I just bit into something really hard!" she cried.

The children's faces lit up instantly.

Mum was pulling something small out of her *samosa*.

"*Subhan Allah!* Mother! It's your ring!" she said in disbelief.

Grandma was so pleased that the ring had been found.

Rahma went to her grandmother and hugged her. "Sorry, Grandma," whispered Rahma. "I think I accidentally dropped your ring in the mixture! Please don't be cross with me."
"There's no harm done," smiled Grandma and she gave Rahma a big hug!

Rahma looked up at Muslimah and chuckled, "I guess we'll always remember this as the *Samosa Eid!*"

Glossary

Adhan – Call to prayer or prescribed worship, said five times a day.

Al-Hamdulillah – Praise be to God.

As-Salamu 'Alaikum – Peace be with you.

Ameen – May Allah accept it.

Ayat-ul-Kursi – Verse of the Throne - Ayah 255 of Surah Al-Baqarah

Day of *Arafat* – The 9th day of Dhul-Hijjah (the Month of Hajj) is called the Day of Arafat, a major pillar of Hajj without which the Hajj is not complete. On this day, Muslim pilgrims gather at Mount Arafat where the Prophet ﷺ delivered his last sermon. Muslims who are not at Hajj are encouraged to fast on this day.

Du'a – Prayer or supplication.

Eid – The day of festival

Eid Gaah – The gathering place where the *Eid* prayer is offered.

Eid Mubarak – A blessed *Eid*.

Eid-ul-Adha – The second major Islamic festival celebrated towards the end of Hajj.

Eid-ul-Fitr – The first major Islamic festival celebrated to mark the end of Ramadan.

Ghusl – Bathing.